about the author

Gary Percesepe is Associate Editor at *New World Writing* (formerly *Mississippi Review*) and a Contributor at *The Nervous Breakdown*. Author of four books in philosophy, Percesepe's poetry, fiction, essays, and interviews have appeared in *Story Quarterly*, *N + 1*, *Salon*, *Mississippi Review*, *The Millions*, *Brevity*, *PANK*, *Wigleaf*, *Metazen*, *The Brooklyner*, and other places.

His collection of short stories, *Why I Did the Grocery Girl*, is forthcoming from Aqueous Books.

Percesepe has taught at Saint Louis University, Wittenberg University, and University of Dayton.

praise for *falling*

Gary Percesepe's literary and film criticism is acute, his fiction startling, evocative, funny, and richly felt, and his poetry meditative and piercing. His political essays are compelling and right—minded, hard by truth to power, and always deserving. I cannot recommend his work highly enough. Everything he writes challenges us in the best possible way.

Frederick Barthelme

Percesepe's poetry seems straightforward but is as complex as flowers, as summer shade and layers of snowfall, available to all but folded around secrets only broken lovers or philosophers grasp, and contained by no borrowed forms but original truths and no meter but the throbs of a heart. He here assays breakfast making and love making and loss and memory and time and husbands and wives and offspring and always, always, the elegance of the line, the object plain or sublime or both, the landscapes of sex, sorrow and high style.

James Robison

Gary Percesepe drops you into an ambiguous world and pulls you back again, still reeling. He does it so deftly, you don't even realize you're bleeding until it's over.

Heather Cox, author of *California King*

Gary Percesepe is absolutely at home writing the voice that fills the poems in *falling*, his latest book. It's a collection of pieces, smoothed by conversation, an easy talk, both natural and telling – filled with rich tapestries of *now*. The book's real gift is its range of imagery, a true presence that is immediate, inviting, and always sharp – "the wide sea / below amalfi" ... "dirty streets of // saint germain–des–pres" ... "cervantes's windmill on fire again" ... "lunches on red checked tablecloths in chelsea" ... "the smell of the bakery in the / lemony light by the harbor" ... "tracks in the black / winter night". In *falling*, Percesepe, whose writing is alive and fresh, nudges, coerces, even pushes the reader to step through the pages into his world. And we do it. The writing is that good.

Sam Rasnake

These poems are simultaneously street–smart and softly lyrical, and they sing the hard–edges of love's brief rapture. From the cafés of Paris to the Nathan's on Coney Island, Percesepe announces himself as our 21st century O'Hara.

Kara Candito, author of *Spectator* and *Taste of Cherry*

From characters in summer suits in Paris, catfish from the Mississippi, baked ziti, the Hudson wearing white, chipped teeth, a single pearl earring, nail polish and frozen pianos, *falling*'s magic icebox spills secrets, joy and heartbreak. Gary Percesepe's poems are unique and original, beautiful and lovely, like the curves of his Manhattan.

Kim Chinquee, author of *Pretty* and *Oh Baby: Flash Fictions and Prose Poetry*

Gary Percesepe's new poetry collection engages, even overwhelms the senses. His poems form vivid, condensed worlds that are – as existence is – both visceral and meditative.

Jen Knox, author of *Don't Tease the Elephants*

What is the sound of Gary Percesepe? It is the sound of "I want to feed you." It is the sound of "I would follow you anywhere." It is also the sound of "falling," "tearing" and "speed." And the sound of "at the back of the mind where we live now." "The news from Brooklyn" resounds from "the tavern of planets," but ultimately it is the sound of "writers in love." It is this sound: "Your milk teeth say no, but I cannot remember a time we didn't imagine that dress, hung in / Kant's closet, a critique of judgment. You." Buy this book. There's heart and mind and music inside.

Bill Yarrow, author of *Pointed Sentences*

Gary Percesepe reaches into what drives the yearning of lost love, hope for love, and the land in between that is both inhospitable and familiar …

Kimberlee Smith

also by Gary Percesepe

fiction

Why I Did the Grocery Girl
forthcoming

itch

What May Have Been:
Letters of Jackson Pollock & Dori G.
with Susan Tepper

philosophy

Ethics: Personal and Social Responsibility in a Diverse World

Free Spirits: Feminist Philosophers on Culture
with Kate Mehuron

Philosophy: An Introduction to the Labor of Reason

Future(s) of Philosophy:
The Marginal Thinking of Jacques Derrida

falling

falling

Gary Percesepe

a Pure Slush book

Pure
Slush

falling and other poems published by Pure Slush, November 2013.

All poems copyright © Gary Percesepe

Front cover design copyright © Pier Rodelon

Author photograph copyright © Jeff Smith

ISBN: 978−1−925101−24−9

All rights reserved.

You can find *Pure Slush* at http://pureslush.webs.com

Copies of all Pure Slush publications can be bought
at http://pureslush.webs.com/store.htm

All queries re *Pure Slush* can be made
via email to edpureslush@live.com.au

for rachel

contents

falling

last night I dreamed I sailed the wide sea

below amalfi   the boat stood on its stern in the

tall swells   there was the smell of oilcloth and fish

nets and the hulk of an old ship laced with

foam and far from shore you came up beside me

a lamppost was there and then it wasn't

snow started to spit and lemons fell

like pale tears while we stood and talked

of all that had passed silent between us

and you laughing suggested we make love

in midair over the angry italian chop

"don't you want to fall a thousand times

to drop into this murderous surf——

on the edge of everything tilted like this

there is always somewhere to fall from."

i want to feed you

hamburgers and fries

slathered in catsup

crisp bacon and eggs

over easy

catfish caught deep

in the channels of

the mississippi   then

baked ziti made from

scratch in my abruzzi

kitchen with garlic i've

sliced thin with a

special razor blade

kept by the toaster and

ricotta cheese i bought

from the little italian

guy on the corner of

arthur avenue who's

been there since fdr

then i'll feed it to you

by the happy forkful

wiping your hungry

mouth with slices of

toasted garlic bread

and a big pour of chianti

till it ran down the slope

of your white shoulders

and reddened your

nipples

which i'd lick with

my greedy tongue

and if i had you i

would go on feeding

till you sped past 100

and you wouldn't stop

eating the chocolate and

hazelnut gelato i'd bring

home from the gelateria

della palma by the pantheon

the pistachio

crowning the cone with cool

green flavor   oh i'd spoon it

into you careening on

now to the poetry which would

dribble down past our belly buttons

winking up at us

and we'd feel as if we'd

awakened on the last day

of our lives at nathan's on

coney island there on the

boardwalk and you know what?

if i had you i wouldn't

share you with anybody.

speed

for Pari

the dream went by this way

i woke and held a cigarette

the hudson wore winter white

you were tinier than imagined

& reached up to hug me on the

corner of west broadway and chambers

we've slept off years

in different cities

a slow burn of days and

speeding nights and

then we were children

in paris

one year the men all dressed in sherbet colored

summer suits of purest linen

it was the year i fell in love with a

hand model

who

wore white gloves during

dinner

removing them only to

rummage through her purse or to

place her fork gently beside

a pale green pistachio cake

as if afraid to sink the

tines deeper

though she got deeper into me

and while I am not complaining

exactly

(because how can you not love a woman

named mazarine)

i already appear to have said

too much

as the french reserve a large category

of thought for *le non dit*

(the unsaid)

which come to think of it might

have made a better title

for this poem

but one hopes not to be found

gauche for observing

that in paris there are

but two ages

youth & decay

and mazarine was youth and i

well

you see

so there she was that

night

with her white gloves and

faint arm hair

and that upward look

that only

young girls have

who so want to please

the woman in my dream

goes barefoot

with one pearl earring

the other has gone missing

she bites my frozen arm

with her chipped tooth

then dips her toes into

blue water lurching

over wet sandbags in

the dirty streets of

saint germain−des−pres

her toes painted a shade

called tomboy no more

look like red penny candy

and she won't give me

back my white oxford shirt

i went home to new york

to escape something but

the woman in my dream

points at the girls in their

summer dresses and is not

interested in my howls or

tears but bites the one apple

left in my backpack and hands me

a perfect snowflake from her purse

she winks from the corner of

my room then pulls the door

shut and sings hey oh

Nail Polish Poems

Tomboy No More

He grabbed one bare foot below her skinny jeans. It felt like a small steel cable, an eel arching its back, finning through a cove.

East Hampton Cottage

Professor of desire, listen! Let me fold you into my arms, feed ten toes to your famished mouth, wear your gaze like a cashmere coat.

Topless and Barefoot

Your milk teeth say no, but I cannot remember a time we didn't imagine that dress, hung in Kant's closet, a critique of judgment. You.

Wife Goes On

In Amagansett, the wooden houses sag. Her sunburned children walk the creaking floor. She rests her feet on the blue sofa. The ocean spills light.

Red—y Set Ex

They married on the 4th of July. The wide lawn was set with white chairs. Alone at her vanity, she stripped polish from reddened nails.

sex at antioch

my friend, a woman who checks her
closet for labels that say large
(thinking that one may have shown up

during the night while she lay sleeping)
picks a popped button off the cold tile floor,
hands it to me, then pulls the tag

off her new dress and says, with no hint
of a smile, the definition of beauty is easy:
it is what leads to desperation

cervantes's windmill on fire again
a suitcase of snow in summer
seven spills you make across her

across the body of your memory.

February Fifth

Later

Much later,
We'll check this date for fleas

The way that police photograph a
Cash register.

We've worked silence over
Like pros, our best work together.

I've done some checking
On your horoscope and see that you're Aquarius, too.

No matter, the future promises to
Be good to us, self—medicated as we are.

And right here it says, "All of this is
Coming your way."

A single teardrop rises into the
Middle air, tired already of its short history.

See that frozen piano?
It's grinning too.

Loosen up, dry your hair,
You can sleep under my bed another year.

She

She plows the carpet with a fast machine.
She buys her clothes at the eight dollar store.
She takes down the garlic from the top shelf.
She bleeds and believes it is for you.

She smiles at her feet in their silvery skates.
She breathes the air you thought you knew.
She knows that her collarbone and wrist are delicate.
She writes to tell you that she cannot write.

She snorts when she laughs which is often.
She lies for fun and shoplifts with abandon.
She undresses with the window open.
She will take you back to your childhood if you let her.

She lives down the hall in a room that is dreamed.
She will walk in her sleep into your life.
She will tell you this was your idea.
She will make you believe it.

She grew out of this corner when all were asleep.
She is the consolation of the merely lonely.
She sees the poor cut down with a sharp grin.
She waltzes on the roof, on the tragic brick

She is never near. What you need
She cancels while looking up from her salad.
She has appeared in Prague, without warning.
She is after us. If you decide

She is necessary it will lead to nowhere.
She has the silent shape of your shadow on the bare wall.
She cries into microphones and applauds despair.
She hungers for more like you.

She is the poetry of failure.
She blinds the stars and beats fire into flakes.

Aerobics 6 P.M.

Dizzy but still alive
Inside this conversation

I ask if you have a sister
And if she'll know me

If I'm with you.
Taking a purple

Scrunchie off your wrist
You pass it through

Your hot hair then
Point to some guy

In the corner whose
Spastic angel arms and

Jacknife jacks are
Comical but unrehearsed

And in the mirror
Now I see your sister

There beside you
Moving backward in a

Perfect glide of unmarked years
Her shining skin

Her smooth dark calves
Her hair holding the light of a

Hundred glistening bodies
The flawless curve of her neck.

Her, dancing.

i would follow you anywhere

anywhere

and if you asked me to stop

would follow the moon behind the cathedral

and in shadow follow the moonlit girls.

writers in love

never meet

but keep each other warm

through long winter nights

texting and emailing and shipping

drafts back and forth in cyberspace

the edits coming back with track changes

and blue lined comments and suggestions

of more if only there were time or the world

wasn't quite so fucked up or there were not

some person in the room peering over the

shoulder to see the unspeakable   the only solace

left to them is to imagine it otherwise and go on

writing   in love but missing the lover   alone only more so

you are a ride on a train

you are a ride on a train

passing grain fields

corner houses blur

the sad gray river; light shifts

to the west and there is something

now the same thing, repeating, repeating

while beneath the floor steel wheels churn

a man says goodbye to his wife

in the dirt yard where sheets flap on

a knotted cord of rope

past the vacant stations we speed

not now never, to stop

like any ordinary heart, pumping

only muscle, tissue & blood

this unknown movement

you passing through me

addicted to a few things

bananafish, snowflakes

women who drink

the lives of painters & shortstops

an irish sweater, ordinary white

a frozen river

women named gabriella

a low cut little black dress

on which my watery eyes linger

lunches on red checked tablecloths in chelsea

talcum powder of a morning

brie, dark chocolate, yellow apples, wood—handled knives

you, barelegged

slinging off shoes

Bananagram

for jessica anya blau

I am only what you are

but we saw and heard so many things

we became as traveling salesmen

who lost sight of the sheep.

Some other holy man will appear to guide you

through small gardens of desire, unspeakable

practices & impossible satisfaction but you

must allow time for exhaustion.

Press more promises upon the faithful, pose

holders, yogis of the heart, it's all yours now

this loss that is continuous will be all yours

and will only increase.

But look! Here is a woman with swell hair

and ample nose slumped and sleepy as James Dean

suddenly awake. Hey, Bananagrams! she says

It's a new game that combines sex & childhood

Yellow, of course, but played with repurposed

Scrabble tiles. She pulls you into a slow

hug and says, I once put a banana in my purse

because art is long and days short

and forgot about it, the banana, that is

until my girlfriend called as I exited the subway at

Grand Army Plaza, so I told her and she said

So much can go wrong with a banana in your purse.

New York, New York

You left your new shoes.—Frank O'Hara

The city's hung in
flashlights. Wizard's
bridges festooned
with garlands for
those who must live
forever. Sun is weak
but no one notices.
Trinity Church alert
like the narrow finger
of God at the head of
the street where money—
men who pray for more
pace nervously for Maria
Bartiromo. Pictures fall
off the wall of a TriBeCa
loft. Bobby DeNiro sighs.
I was too young to lose
my virginity to the girl
from Virginia that I
met at the Waldorf so
instead I smiled and
stood next to her on
the choir risers. I miss
the Horn and Hardart
automat, the camel
smoke curling out
of the sign in Time's
Square. Twice a day

traffic comes to a com—
plete halt in honor of
Robert Moses on the
LIE. I don't remember
her name, the girl I
mean, but if you see
her would you tell her
for me that it's OK to be
an out of towner when
you look like Catherine
Deneuve. And that I'll
wait for her on the Circle
Line, Pier 83, West 42nd
Street, she can cab it
but don't forget the tip.

something

it was the unexpectedness of our music

the way the baleful stars withdrew

when i walked you to the subway

the shattered city hissed in time.

for sara on her thirty–seventh birthday

the instant you arrive you go missing

your own private bergeron

family images show

you standing slender hunched half naked

pieces of you

folded into corners of every

spilled holiday

even the

pitchy silences are being

added to our bill−−

here:

have a glass of something

this is your newly cut hair

you will hear a city

Question

The eagerness of objects to be what we are afraid to do cannot help but move us.—Frank O'Hara

Aren't you acting terribly pre—9/11?

Someone has to smile at her as she

comes back from the bathroom. I can't

say I'm sorry. Do you think everything

can stay the same like a photograph?

When you smile airplanes go off course.

Thundering windows of hell will you

forever speak Rudy Giuliani noun verb 9/11?

Or pocket your carpenter's pencil? Clear the

room of smoke? Shit, the soup is on fire.

My father is at the back door with the roses.

The strange hills are still warm from the

feet of worn travelers. And still the manna

falls. If you were an enormous bullet you could

lodge here in my open shirt. Downstairs,

we scream and wash our hair.

spill

i settled in with a sandwich

some grapes in a deep dish

and a cup of minestrone

from the magic icebox

locating some cream for the

strawberries and started in on a

fresh pitcher of tequila sunrise when

uh oh   my negative capabilities

acted up again   a fine dust

formed in my throat and my

teeth started humming the ramones

was that emily bronte galloping by

on horseback dragging charlotte on the

pink lawn   then the tv came on and

zooey deschanel was singing in another

bad movie   her fingertips dipped in

ripe nostalgia and the smell was atrocious

& then pretty soon six purple pointed scorpio tails

were armed and aimed at my aquarian throat

and just when i thought it couldn't get

worse cameron diaz attempted an accent

and i began to think that this was all

a party thrown by those festive chipmunks in the

neighborhood who quoted pascal and insisted on

raison d'être for breakfast and then my lord!

eleanor roosevelt waddled up with franklin

all smiles and top−hatted, his long cigarette holder

canted at a precarious angle and whacking

dick cheney with his cane and one perfect tear

formed on my lashes and fell into my soup

and i managed a smile

and came again to love the lunatic world

with its cute baby chiggers and chattering lemurs

and old sol's beard of snow and all those happy

bris goers in summer and even ritual circumcision

seemed then not so bad an idea so i clucked to my

intern and she settled over mine and i wondered how

i'd snapped into that mood anyway and where it had gone

as i added to the cream but threw away the soup

then climbed the high ladder to the attic watching the

intern's bubble ass rise higher and right here is where i

remembered how my old nona used to tell me sonny boy!

doncha know only way you chase dat memory of a woman

is with another woman?   and then we were at the top and my

intern pulled the ladder up behind us and said hot damn

where's the cherry bombs?

still life

all life is one

but there are these

fragments to consider

yet it is

always an

accident that saves us

life is a single page

an hour badly spent or

maybe one long afternoon

of lost keys

it is someone we have

never seen coming to us

as a meal prepared

tiny feet

in a battery park fountain

wet & tan

holding your body close

to learn how you breathe

everything

is practiced through the body

these are the real hopes of man

the sky exhausted &

bled by the early june heat

our lives of

beautiful disorder

each wooden spoon or

cracked plate or

bowl of cut crystal

the polished pear

in this comfortable room

every observed

object passes

into quiet ruin

if I had you

outside those fiery windows

the city collapses in meteors of light

your eyes brief coals

stoke the flame

spur your flanks till

ashes loft brightly into black heaven

smoldering tongues

our night of fire

pages, burning

the tearing

for danielle

something so small beneath the big bright sky

stands erect

in echo park

leaking tears from pores

from eyes & open mouth

all of us raining

everyone crying

soaking in the cruel los angeles light

watching her puddle the parched ground

rivulets of salt and bone

you imagine a new river to carry you both

to the pacific

past the vacant apartment buildings

toward the ghostly canyon

how many steps to the sea

how many graves

to ride this way

she can get you somewhere

a road trip through the painted desert

the amphitheatre rock of ouray &

unwashed backs of tractor trailers

lit like circus squares in the thin blank night

alone

from fingertips

all of us dying

you think

but now you see tied around her tiny finger

a string

and knotted to tie her

to what we'll pull behind us

the shattered sound of summer thunderstorms

tearing beneath us

she's sliced

the road

as we speed back by

fragments

for sara

because the only song that comes to mind is taps

you lie in bed

in a room full of secrets

the brooklyn bridge lit early against the soiled sky

beyond it the curve of manhattan

now every day is a little bit fucked

despite moon bright frozen trees

now is the winter of our discontent

one poet said

tears   the aftermark of almost too much love

guest   that's all that remains of husband now

but why do i linger on

i lived on air

yet we go on talking

while overhead the great black flood

polishes the most distant stars

counterclockwise

the ways we miss our lives

     are life

but today I remember the

     way a woman

looks when she lies fully

     clothed in bed

her face upturned to

     the ceiling

and the way she turns

     just her head

to follow as you move in

     beside her

and that way she looks

     beneath you

as your head hovers above

     her lips

for just a second as you

   lock eyes

to be sure she is willing to receive

   what is

coming and cannot be stopped

   but why

must we watch the snow fall into

   the fire

or come to trust only the saddest

   moments of

our lives or raise a glass to only

   small pleasures

when she in your memory

   pulled your

head into her strong hands

   and turned

over onto her small hip so that you

   faced each

other and your eyes were level

     the way

you always wanted to be with

     a woman

level—eyed and face to face

     and then

she says hey you what else you got

     for me

but now i see how all things

     false fall

from the dead   the slow voice

     of ruin.

Love, An Inquiry

Q: We hate to ask.

A: I know. It's OK.

Q: So is *counterclockwise* a poem about divorce?

A: It is, among other things.

Q: And do you love her, even so?

A: I do.

Q: Is it possible to stay too long in a marriage?

A: Of course.

Q: Do you know it at the time?

A: Not always.

Q: Why do you stay too long?

A: Because you remember and because you are afraid.

Q: Can you overcome your fear?

A: Not easily.

Q: How did you do it?

A: Supposing that I have?

Q: Yes.

A: I didn't. I stayed too long.

Q: But she was fine? When you left, I mean?

A: She was, as it turns out, but I couldn't have known it at the time.

Q: What is the mystery of marriage?

A: There is no mystery to marriage. Only questions you do not know the answers to.

Q: So you could have left earlier and she would have been fine?

A: I'm not saying that. I'm not a big believer in fine, as a rule.

Q: What do you believe in, then?

A: Oranges. Root beer floats. A hot bowl of pasta and a jug of water at my writing desk. The moon's backwash hanging like a hairnet over the stadium. A ghost train lit against the snow shrouded moor.

Q.   I believe in these questions.

A: And the translation of all things into their opposites. Every virtue is a glittering vice. Every cup drips air, and all things are in blinding motion. Even the earth, though we forget to feel it.

Q: Do you believe in being in love?

A: Not especially. Another form of narcissism, perhaps. In any case, a cultural product of the West, like capitalism. Marketed as such by the Mad Men. February 14, and so forth.

Q: But you believe in love.

A: Yes, of course.

Q: How many times have you been in love?

A: Four times. Each time an earthquake. Though there are different measuring systems, different orders of magnitude.

Q: But you have loved many more?

A: Yes. Men, women, dogs, cities, continents, convertibles. The English word is weak.

Q: Is there an end to love?

A: Yes, but we cannot know it. We love to our limit but then find that our capacity increases. We always surprise ourselves in love. The capacity to be surprised is an element of goodness.

Q: What is love, then?

A: Torment & misery. A hunger. A violent upheaval. A lifting up and out of the ordinary order of things.

Q: Should we seek it?

A: It seeks us. Though some are never found.

Q: Some say love is eternal. And when a marriage fails, love
      is injured, perhaps fatally.

A: These are the ones who do not believe in their own
      humanity. Because marriage does not endure is no reason
      to hold temporality suspect. If contingency, chaos,
      sorrow and disorder are held to be invalidating, then
      nothing real succeeds.

Q: Can one love too early in life?

A: Clearly.

Q: What then?

A: Pray to endure.

Q: Can one love too late?

A: Never.

when it became time to go

lamps are lit

where are you?

the last time

i saw you

the tent came un—pegged

soon we were sliding

out to sea

a shelf of iceberg surfaced

from the inky waves

i sped to the other side

of the boat

where it began to rain

you went back to your

box of paints

now I occupy my share

of days

light leaches upward and rolls

into dark clouds

i adjust my eyes

stitching the wilderness together

and wait for the

night train

the door is shutting & of course i

know *how* to say

i love you

but the stain

why does it spread to

all the beautiful parts?

and look

here comes queen mab

with her dream elixir

to make me believe

you had become the

complete vision

of all that I had missed

dreams are like that

making your apartment door as

white as snow

the beloved past decays

i am a keeper of drawings

and silent sonatas

now others will have to

believe for me

there are always more worlds

to travel

but when it became time to go

neither of us would leave

before the other

divorce

the story continues

but without us

as main characters

there was a

truth to our lives

that went beyond facts

i want a life with

clean sheets

gleaming glasses

the broad atlantic

starched white napkins

a wood fire &

view to the east

a breakfast of

chocolate & oranges

the courage to

live when one's best

days are past

but for now

a spoon of tea

an empty cup

this worn toothbrush

seem as strange as a

suitcase of snow

Found Art

after john hawke

After he died you found a photograph. A composition of bathing
girls. Giant boulders for a sheltering solid wall, still water rippling
as with light on oil, the old white hull of a sailboat bisecting the
photograph from left to right. And sprawling on the deck of the
weathered hull, the girls. Five slender ropes rise to the right of
the center toward an invisible boom, two thicker ropes slope
carelessly from the stern of the hull into the water, sagging,
bearing no weight. All clear, black and white, sensible at first
glance. But the girls, those symbols of summer, are uncountable.
The snapshot cropped so that above the hull and girls and across
the width of the picture only a little of the rocks is shown—there
is twice as much water below the girls and hull as expanse of
rocks above them. The water looks painted rather than snapped
by a young artist, one perhaps my age, using a box camera. All is
arranged so as to concentrate on the sprawling girls. But how
many? It is a matter of wit as much as math or memory. For the
viewer's first appreciative moments their number is not a
question, as other incongruities enter the picture. Who snapped
it and to what purpose and why has it lain hidden in this folder
all these long years in the hot attic of this empty summer house?
Another look and with it the certainty of five girls in the picture.
Four lie with their legs hanging over the edge of the hull, behind
them sits another reading a book. Five. Well, yes. But there is
one more pair of legs close together—crossed at the ankles in
fact—and dangling down toward the water precisely in the

middle of the snapshot. The legs of the four present to the viewer listless near verticals that catch the light and the viewer's eye as well, the pair of legs crossed at the ankles is hidden behind the thighs and calves of the middle two, hardly more than respose in dark shadow. But wait! A portion of a head shows behind and resting on the shoulder of the girl who usurps the center of the picture. A portion of a leg rises out of the left–hand edge of the picture, there is a scraped knee floating upwards to the right, another white sphere, again on the left, reveals itself as the cranium of a head in a white skull–tight bathing cap. And another head rests on the turned–up hip of the girl reading a book. So that the number has now changed to nine, sprawled in this summer still life. But why did you not show me this picture, father, or name the sorority or tell me who the girl was in the center, the star, the one you composed the picture around, or why my eye drifts to the left, to that one perfect leg whose scraped knee I would enter the picture to kiss again and again?

it gets dark early here

nothing is happening

and happening fast

the moon is a sharp saw

for cutting dreams back

everyone is scaling down

or so I've heard

even my poet friends

are pinching commas

i keep walking into the wrong room

lots of pages in this warehouse

by afternoon we were soaked

was it only yesterday i hit that home run?

suddenly everyone's a big shot

love in boots

passes swiftly

on superior planets

the reception is better

but if it's a timetable you're looking for

look out!

well, that was the local

it may have been what she wanted all along

a scene from a foreign movie set to classical

music, french perhaps, or italian, where the lovers

pose by a balustrade or walk among statuary

in the lobby before war separates them or the

guests scatter for a fox hunt.

it was as if she had brewed a pot of supremely

strong coffee for breakfast and set out two

italian pastries to transport them back to

amalfi and the smell of the bakery in the

lemony light by the harbor in june

and she watched his gaze as it traveled

her face until he noticed something different

about his wife   the shape of her hair   the new

scarf she wore   the book whose title she hid while

she read long into the night

that made him realize she was having an affair

and then it was snowing

and he won't forget how she told him

he made her feel beautiful in the snow

her lashes wet   her face upturned to his

hungry mouth   and he realized what he

wanted was what he thought that he wanted—

to sleep beside her one last sexless night

to delight in the curve of her back

the slope of her slender shoulder

the way the dirty moon hid in clouds

of night   the way her child's barrette

slipped out of her hair while she slept

at coney island

you

who never arrived

have we lost even the morning air

we drove in silence

yellow fog

swallowed the headlights

atlantic wind

tangled your dark hair &

blued your watery eyes

damp air leaked onto

boardwalk faces

the day you disappeared

Notes From Underground

The end is rehearsed over and over;

in a world without heaven all is farewell.

There's a stretch of ice and snow ahead

visible from your basement window.

You sit on the big bed billing hours while

outside under the great sky grief falls like leaves.

In the crooked streets of the suburbs women are

strung like Christmas lights on telephone poles

their heads positioned like satellite dishes

tuned to imaginary planets.

I want to sit on the roof of your old building high

above the Hudson and take one last ride with you

beyond the papery Palisades, past the tall ships

dozing in the harbor to see Lady Liberty, who looks

like she's put on weight and donned a pair of glasses

to peer over at Jersey, squinting at the barest watery wave,

scribbling dissolving messages on her ten foot tablet,

raising her stony arm in salute.

At the Back of the Mind
Where We Live Now

At dawn we meet in fibrous shadows

Each thought a sinewy tree

Connected to every feeling

In the forest.

It's where we meet to keep

From meeting again.

We do not touch.

We do not repeat what

Others say about us.

Nor what we used to say about

Each other. No gaping

Holes in the sky

Remain to be healed

No stairs to climb to closed off rooms.

We palm the moisture sliding off the

Slippery bark.

The lidless eye of morning,

Watches. And when

We sigh it is

With relief

As if to say

Enough.

In These Rooms

for pari

On a day when the October light poured through holes

in the clouds, when the world was blank and the air raw

we came running to these rooms from bordering planets.

Winter settled in and the frost deepened. Snow fell faintly.

What was unspoken between us continued as before. I orbited

in the Miami River valley, you tanned and did hot yoga in Jersey.

After my divorce we joked Ohio is like Jersey, only more so.

You found me the perfect little house on the railroad tracks,

Promising to visit but we both knew better. We cancelled Christmas

that year, but watched *The Good Wife* together by phone, tracking

Alicia Florrick's bangs. *Stacy's Mom* played in the car we bought;

your children howled with glee. Quiet episodes of longing on the phone, then you'd say, knock it off. It made me laugh, to think you knew me

that well. And loved me, anyway. Once, you called at 3 am wondering

what was your five year plan? Where would you be, where would you

live, what the fuck was the plan? I was asleep, but listened gamely.

Then said: Marry me. Through my open window I watched the

great star fields splinter as seconds stretched to minutes of stunned

silence. Then these stupid tears. Boy and girl, we walked back up the

poet's hill. While the north wind pressed against your mother's house,

I cleaned the refrigerator and checked my Facebook messages.

If the future has any waves we'll ride one in. For now: these rooms,

this marble moon, your nippled dog in bed, grinning.

the news from brooklyn

last night the ghost train

roared by and I saw the faces

of the newly dead

and the blissfully happy.

I thought of my wife alone

in the big old house in the

last hour of light.

The house has gaping

cavities, my furniture

extracted by men

in uniform bearing clip

boards and tattooed grocery lists.

Outside in the city

huge tires of buses

sticky on the hot pavement

peel like pus—filled scabs.

I miss her occasional

ordinary sounds, the

ambient noise of someone

living a life not mine

drawers opening and

closing, the clanging of

spoons, the sound of crockery

banging in carried boxes.

The train passes and I see

her rip her pale necklace

to small pieces & watch

myself lift from the filthy

floor a spent yellow metro card

that I flip casually into the trash,

along with this old newspaper

the borough's life in black & white.

The Night Train

for J

I

The night train stopped at my house.

It sat on the tracks in the black

winter night, waiting.

I was lying in bed looking at a picture

of a woman whose cancerous breasts

had sent her lover packing

but not before penning

a short note which he thoughtfully

pinned to her bed cover.

Her hair came out in clots

that felt like straw fed to

galloping ghost horses

ridden by radiated toy soldiers

and her life sped backwards until she was

 nine again, which was when

she sent the train for me.

II

It was nearly midnight. The train stood high as my house. The house is fastened to the track in the back of my yard. Out front, on a street which curves east, then suddenly north, with crazy half blocks shooting off like broken ribs, stand houses so small they look like tokens on a Monopoly board. The train shuddered in the black night. I went to my back door. Overhead, the stars were shining. The engineer turned on the powerful headlight of the locomotive. A bell began to toll. A jackrabbit, startled, ran into a bush. The train began to move. It was then that I knew she'd sent it for me.

far from us

for patti smith and robert mapplethorpe

i picture you with a star at your foot

making you cornell boxes with colored

string, paper lace, discarded rosaries and

black pearls, a visual poem written for one

i'd give you an italian vase if I thought it'd

help, but I've discarded your spell for prayer

long ago I figured out that you were my twin

but we shuttle back and forth like the ferryman's

children, across four states of non–being, across

our river of tears, telling our stories like wendy

entertaining the lost children of neverland

and baby, you know what? it's not us.

patti, did art get us?

for patti smith & robert mapplethorpe

often as i lie awake i wonder   are you awake too?

      we never had any children, he said ruefully

that summer i cried so much that robert called me soakie

      robert, dying: creating silence

nineteen i was   i'd given my baby up for adoption

      why can't i write something that would awaken the dead?

i first saw you sleeping on a simple iron bed   pale & slim

      there is strength in blackness   pure hearts are kin

bare–chested with strands of beads below his chin

      will you write our story?   no one but you can

he opened his eyes and smiled   his shepherd hair   his mass of curls

      do you want me to? i never heard him speak again

that night in brooklyn we'd looked at books on dali and surrealism

      our work was our children

wordless we absorbed each other's thoughts and fell asleep at dawn

    he was a man but in his presence i still felt like a girl

we stayed together all summer, nothing spoken   but understood

    we were hansel & gretel in the black forest world

at the whitney we only had money for one ticket, so

    i stayed outside and lit a cigarette and awaited your report

we dreamed our work would be displayed there one day

    we buried him at the whitney museum at the blue hour

but of all your work, you are still the most beautiful

    the most beautiful of all

little emerald bird   wants to fly away

    it is true i heard god is where you are

little emerald soul   must you say goodbye?

    if i cup my hand could i make him stay?

little emerald eye

    we must say goodbye

January 1

I sat in bed looking out at the empty street. Like bran accumulating in whorls on the rutted earth or cats circling milk, my thoughts were wanton. Someone kept calling but the satellite was defective. I'd severed links to the past, no crisis for the mailman. Boundaries, you cannot really have enough. It was as though my doctor pronounced me ready for a bout of amnesia just when I was ready to put the gloves on again. I couldn't begin to give an account of the latest days. On the radio, someone was saying something about how no two people could agree about the meaning of a sentence, how nothing really is required of us. I wanted to pound a three penny nail into the speakers. There's a crack in every conversation. Meanwhile, the sky out my window has no color. Blackbirds pass overhead like punctuation. There's a feeling like rain. Once, in high school, I knew where I wanted to go. This was during my senior year. In class, our history teacher apologized profusely for what was coming. Every coastline would change, he said. It was the first encouraging thing he'd said all year. The road is made by walking. I stood up and moved toward the door. I wanted to return to the refectory.

January 2

for jeanne

You turned sixty today.

The last three years passed to ash

from lavender.

Thoughts of January are long thoughts.

And you were beautiful

in the maple shade where we left you.

You always complained that Christmas

ruined your birthday,

sister.

But where are you, really?

Do you have your own house, now?

It snowed here today.

I met a woman, does that surprise you?

You'd like her,

you'd like the way she loves me.

But I understand how gypped you felt.

Fifty—seven times!

But where is that boy

who waited for you to get out of

the bathroom while you put on

your makeup?

I was always a little behind you

but I'm

moving faster now.

haiku

for pari

kids on the white beach

balance balls, roll a stroller

sea gulls crazed with flight

black waves of mussels

sawyer watches his sister

sun sinking westward

a montclair book store

you sit reading a big book

glasses freckles nose

white connecticut

house with hidden memories

i want to hold you

raspberry nipples

my shocked fingers hesitate

long hot kisses heal

if grief could burn out

we would stay up all night long

stirring the coals cool

Patrick Melrose Reflects

Snowflakes like white gloves cover the cold earth. It is
December again. My house—my ex wife's house—is lit for the
season, a candle for each room, seventeen in all. Or eighteen, the
math of things is always in question. Fuzzy as these snowflakes,
which continue to fall while I write inside this Moleskin with
the wrong pen. We were married for twenty—five years,
twenty—six if you count the year on the couch. Which I don't,
usually. I stand outside my house—well, her house, now. I'm
trying to hold this broken umbrella and keep writing, bear with
me. To think of the things one has done for intimacy is
embarrassing, earth flying over your shoulder. There are good
women who wanted to give the care one never had. They must
be tortured into letting you down in order to show that they
cannot really be trusted. And then there are the bad women who
save you time. It helps to alternate between these two broad
categories. Ha ha. What's that movie that ends with a stucco
house in a big square with a central garden and a woman in the
window three stories above, beautiful, available, and mentally ill?
Hoping and moping, moping and hoping. Who was it who said
that romance was where love is most under threat, not where it
is likely to achieve its highest expression? Well, OK, that was
me. To be able to sit in the same room with oneself requires real
effort. Not to mention holding this damn umbrella. Someone has
thrown a 7—Eleven Big Gulp cup on the white lawn. The cup
has filled with snow. None of this faintly falling, falling faintly
shit, this is a Nor'easter. Still, the cup stands by the iron gate like
a soldier at his post, or a husband at his job. Ha. That's
Kierkegaard in the ethical stage. A stage I apparently skipped.

I was a child here for a long time. But it's embarrassing to be so deluded one runs from the delusion like an out of control lecture. The days scud past like tumbleweed in a tornado. Someone said how sad that everything must change, and yet what a relief, too. Otherwise we'd have only looking forward to look forward to. The tree that stood on this lawn is no longer here, as if to prove it occupied a different slot in the history of objects. I lack a lectern for this. Still, each event becomes a forbidden meaning of thunder and curdled white milk and invoices continue to be forwarded to the wrong department. Birds settle in small coves in the eaves of the house. In the morning they'll be screaming for food.

You Are a River in Winter

A thought can turn you.

Snow melts in the piney

woods. A shade pulled

at dusk reappears each

morning as blind hope.

That you will call or

Write. But you won't.

We lit the last house

on fire.

Since you left I've been

confused about moonlight.

It reflects off the broken

glass of this champagne

flute I smashed in the

kitchen.

You run past the bare

farmhouses. Cheekbones

and tall black boots,

ribbed leggings winter white

sweater dress with lattice

work. Another sighting

another restaurant

the eternal recurrence

of the same.

I wanted you.

The two of you,

The one who kissed

me and the one who

left. She had her

reasons. But I could

have loved you. I could

have really loved you.

I'm saying: I wanted

you. I would have

given anything.

Us

I was thinking of you

the other day;

about the parts

that were yours

in us

and how those

parts are the

ones

i don't get

staged

our immediate universe is like the scenery of theatre

things have changed

we've come back into fashion

just by showing up

a spade has come to turn us.

we get all the dim light we

need   tip your cap,

bow & hold out your arms

i'm naked now

and ready for breakfast

for the moment

regret nothing

The Tavern of Planets

One hangs by the broken front door,

axis shuddering under the weight of

dwarf years.

It greets each regular; the

red eye opens and closes

in tired recognition.

There are disturbances on its cool surface:

popping storms & electrical outbursts

heard above the din of Monday Night Football.

A fine dust covers us, our

cratered days & cragged faces;

multivalent hearts

lined with phosphorus hopes,

we await the ceremonial new moon,

or someone to sit by us to tell us the

necessary lies.

Later, we swing past battered

moonlight in ordinary orbits out the door

Which is no less broken than

before, satellites of

desire at the Tavern of Planets.

Back in the News

In the republic of other things fame dies in a day.

What about the geckos who don't do commercials?

There is always another carnival barking.

We look like late foliage by now.

Normally I'd climb you like a comma.

We're trapped between underperforming texts.

Ankle over to our affiliate they're interviewing the prophet Absurdia.

Folk watch Fox like mice behind the grill.

Seems like we've been here a long time.

Look out, here comes another suffering update.

We're a few marsupials short of a menagerie.

Spin again.

Sisters

What Did We Fight Over?

Makeup and clothes, boys sometimes.

The car, the prom, the right to—

But clothes, mostly.

What Were Our Names?

Vanessa and Amelia,

Charbe and Rhonda,

Karen and Beth,

Gabriella and Lisa.

Where Are We Now?

Rome and Amsterdam,

New York and Nairobi.

Ohio. Might as well be Jersey.

What Do We Do?

Stare at bridges

And planes that bank

Overhead. Signal turns,

Leave vapor trails. At

Jobs clerking, counting, typing,

Phoning, joking, drinking,

Eating, undressing, texting.

Zumba in the half light of

Vacant winter nights.

What Do We Hope For?

The swift turnover of

Days, the weekend music

The baby's breath soft in the

Crib by our nighttime

Lips, moist with hope.

Why Did We Do It?

The soft rain told us otherwise

But we went on chirping,

Oblivious. The layered

Days concealed a lot.

We thought the kingdom of

Lies far from us. Husbandry

We thought we had mastered.

What Did Our Mothers Tell Us?

That we'd be happy, sober, sorry,

Broke, miserable, too far away,

Too close, lousy with money,

Prettier in pink, better with

Bangs, without. Small breasted but

Kind. And to call, mostly.

What Do We Resolve?

To be understood. To sleep.

Keep more in mind by tomorrow.

To stop wearing toy wristwatches.

To smooth the

Wrinkles of days that pass

Like silent trains through

Backyards we meant to tend.

canto della terra

for tara

shouldered awake as

      at first communion

           the darkened woods

                                  groaned below

    a hill   that marked mid—journey

the end of

           sky above

                      your appearance

      so sudden

eyes   the deepest

                wish of blue

rays   of bright planet

            to move   the sun

            earth

    and all

stars

Solstice

for kimberlee

It was one of those summer nights in Amagansett when the air
was filled with the faint smell of the sea and oranges rested in
bowls of cut glass on checked tablecloths that lifted at the corners
in the gentle breeze. It was nearly solstice. Frankie sat on the
sofa, reading. Her hair hung dark in a long column between her
white shoulders. The dishwasher was emptied. Spoons were in
the drawer. The children were down for the night. Golden light
filled the house, reflecting off the polished hardwood floor. In
early summer it was still possible to think a wide umbrella,
lightly—battered fried chicken, tomatoes, cheese, French bread,
cucumbers, butter, bread, wine, white skies and fragrant cigars
could bring them all to shore. The great trees sighed. Empty
now, the beach was endless. White caps flashed in the distance.
The gray Atlantic swelled. Voices drifted from a party at the
house next door. Frankie reached for the princess phone. She
swung her boyish hips and faced the green lawn that led to the
water. "You know, he is such a good father," she said. Her
husband was part of a foursome at Maidstone. There would be
drinks in the lounge after the round. She tightened his club
sweater around her, cinching the belt with her free hand. "But
that's not what stops me," she continued. Frankie twisted the
cord around her hand. She gripped the edge of the coffee table
with her bare toes. It was a rented house. They had to be out
tomorrow, their anniversary. Her twin sons slept in a pink
canopy bed. Finally she said, "It's his damned optimism. I could

never compete with that. He has a surgeon's faith in good outcomes. He treats everyone like one of his patients. I have to let him save me once a day or he's impossible. It's like living with God, if you can imagine God in the Hamptons." She scratched her thin neck with a long fingernail, then picked at a mosquito bite. She placed her finger in her mouth to taste the metallic blood. "Yeah," she said. "It's his optimism that's most depressing. Am I whining again?" Assured on the other end that she was not, she continued. "It's freakish. I hate him for hoping, so what does that make me?" On the other end, in the sweltering city, her lover listened, bored.

Hurricane Love

"Because of the women and how the men struggle to hear inside them"—
Jack Gilbert, Gift Horses

Sandy lashed the coast as I idled in Ohio. TV anchormen hung
like human barometers in angry Atlantic swells. Wharf water
poured down subway station steps onto third rails which, let's
face it, I knew something about. And there was my mother to
think about, without power or heat and huddled in bed with the
covers drawn tight around her, but also Kate, whose raspy voice,
once a siren, sounded more plaintive than seductive, amped by
eight luxury speakers in my speeding BMW, asking me why,
what was I thinking, insisting that this too was a mistake. Pari
was on the phone next with news that Route 9 was closed and
how she'd been driving around for two hours trying to get a
prescription filled and by the way, there is no gasoline,
anywhere, is beYOND, her Jersey voice more guttural than
usual, and by now I was crunching through hurricane snow and
sudden ice at a Sunoco station in the mountains of eastern
Pennsylvania, which was amusing in a way, and fielding another
call from Kate, tottering on a tirade, when I got to thinking
about Janette, safely bedded in Toronto, and kind of missing her
if you want to know the truth and oh shit, there is a tree in the
right lane of Interstate 95 so I swerve into the middle lane and
look into my rear view mirror in time to see Sandy toss the tree
onto an overpass. And Governor Christie is screaming at morons
on the radio and Chris Matthews is leaning forward on MSNBC
about how this plays in Peoria for Romney when Kate interrupts

with another bulletin about us, how there is no us, and who am I to argue? And Pari is begging can I get Eliot's prescription filled somewhere, and where in the hell am I anyway? And right here is when I realize my Navigation System has detoured me to the surface roads of North Philly and no light in this city is working and the wind has bent storefront signs and not even a bar is open for a midnight gamble and I am now going south to get north in a ninety mile an hour gale and the ramp to the interstate is closed and look who drove up the off ramp to go backwards into a super storm. The storm inside me will subside in time, and will return. No one knows all about us, though some know plenty. Who could have predicted I'd meet a woman in time for my February birthday who'd remind me of that night, a Jersey girl (of course!) with the temperament of a Russian spy, who by herself would blow out all my candles, her blonde hair loose against a fur hood, her long body pressed to mine for what seemed a fortnight. She'd stand glaring in the faint starlight of a hotel room in Soho insisting she hadn't given me her room number. It's a big job, inside, she'd later say. Well, yes. We'd made plans to meet at the *Museo de la Tortura* in Siena, toasting Dante and stopping for drinks some long summer evening. *Io venni in loco d'ogne luce muto, che mugghia come fa mar per tempest, se da contrary venti e combattuto.* Meanwhile, back in Ohio, the arrangement she sent stands in its vase on my bedroom dresser, the flowers keeping me awake all night with the sound of their petals, falling.

Half Loaf

"The guests arrived at the summer house."—Pushkin

This snowy morning I'm soothing myself

with bacon, which I haven't tried in years.

Hot chocolate, china. Why not. And this wee bread I

found at Kroger packaged in half a loaf for divorced men.

No woman to remove my bandana, or point her fork at me.

No one to ask, after a violent fall on black ice bounced

my head off the pavement: Baby, do I need a

Cat Scan? Ha! she'd say, picking at her pale lipstick

You *def* need a brain scan. No seriously, I'd say,

do you think I should go to the emergency room?

And she'd reach over in bed, take my hand, and say

firmly, I'm your emergency, baby. I'm it. Right here.

What Little of Her

for rachel

Whatever you've imagined has already been lost. What little of her I've stored in my body I feel sing through me, a soft rising alto. Pale thin feet, toes glistening in my mouth, the last refrain of her hymn of nevertheless. Picture what no longer arrives at my back door. Inside, her young mouth, the way she offers each of her descending breasts, her rainy hair and girlish hands, each memory erasing the last. At twenty−two she carried it all away. Ecstasy is a long loneliness, mister. Brooklyn Bridge jumpers have time for keys and coins to fall from pockets. I'm a paper boat sailing through Central Park. Silent, sinking.

More Abandoned Sentences

Trains ran into the night. By morning it was over. Several pigs entered the open window. The light felt slightly used. We worked ourselves into another corner. February frays worse than other months. My lover's feet are nothing like this. Some rooms face the ocean. Your crackpot therapist called again. This clock is always wrong. Now, I just sit quietly in the attic. See, this is why I never sing to you! Lady Gaga was awarded intelligence. Suddenly we were low on hope. She practices husbandry and deep yoga. Biscuits were plentiful. Everyone ran toward the fruit bowl at once. The dog smiled from the corner of the picture. It's time to say something about the winter garden. Frogs jut from pinecones. There were so many things I wanted to say. Butter these bananas. We could all be caviar. I'm double parked in Bolivia. Bats dripped hair onto startled footmen. Not you, again, she said.

acknowledgments

Grateful acknowledgment is made to the following magazines, where these poems were first published:

falling, *Atticus Review*

i want to feed you, in paris, far from us, when it became time to go, you are a ride on a train, Patrick Melrose Reflects, Hurricane Love, *U City Review*

speed, *Four Paper Letters*

the woman in my dream, *Foundling Review*

Nail Polish Poems, *Nail Polish Stories*

sex at antioch, February Fifth, Aerobics 6 P.M., *Mississippi Review*

Bananagram, Notes From Underground, *Fwriction*

New York, New York, *Prick of the Spindle*

Sisters, *Metazen*

something, *PANK*

Question, More Abandoned Sentences, *Dogplotz*

the tearing, at coney island, counterclockwise, Love, An Inquiry, *The Nervous Breakdown*

fragments, *Pirene's Fountain*

divorce, *THIS Literary Magazine*

Found Art, *Used Furniture Review*

patti, did art get us?, the news from brooklyn, still life, *The Brooklyner*

The Night Train, *Train Write*

Half Loaf, *Structo Magazine*

Back in the News, *Elm Leaves Journal*

other books from *Pure Slush*

Visit the *Pure Slush Store* at
http://pureslush.webs.com/store.htm

itch
by Gary Percesepe
ISBN: 978−1−925101−21−8
Originally published November 2013

Gary Percesepe drops you into an ambiguous world and pulls you back again, still reeling. He does it so deftly, you don't even realize you're bleeding until it's over.
Heather Cox, author of *California King*

Gary Percesepe writes beautiful, vivid stories with the intensity and brevity of a man on the run. His fiction lights up the page with incredible bursts of poetry, passion, and pain channeled through characters whose names we rarely catch. In just a few short pages, Percesepe captures entire worlds of emotion − all of it so true and real, it's impossible to look away. *Jessica Anya Blau*

itch is a shrewd, swift−moving collection about urges, obsessions, and the energy of desire. Gary Percesepe's stories work together to expose and examine a curious cycle − the way our reality drives our fantasies and our fantasies influence our reality. *Jen Knox*

The Merrill Diaries
by Susan Tepper

ISBN: 978−0−9922778−2−6
Originally published July 2013

The Merrill Diaries follows a quirky young woman running from a couple of doozy marriages but mainly from herself. Humor as well as pathos are discovered as our narrator opens up to the world, takes risks, and learns. The language is whip smart, the characters live and breathe on the page   *Bonnie ZoBell*

The Merrill Diaries takes you on a wild ride ... This novel in stories is the end of innocence and the start of "the broken tracks, the roads where the river has flooded over."   *Gloria Mindock*

The language is spare and intense getting quickly into the staccato rhythms of Merrill's slap−dash life. Great fun, yet sad too.   *Gay Degani*

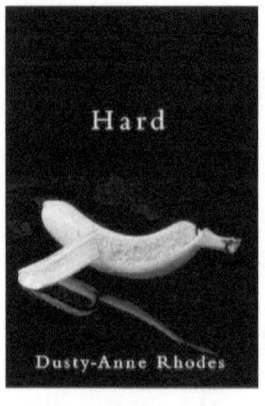

Hard
by Dusty−Anne Rhodes

ISBN: 978−1−291−37970−9
Originally published April 2013

Dusty−Anne Rhodes' non−fiction has earned praise for its honesty and quirky ability to see beneath the surface and bring out the human in its subjects.

Her vignettes explode and when they are done, our familiar furniture is not in the same place. For that matter, neither are we.   *Tim Page*

Her empathy for the emigrant, the downtrodden and the faceless, shines through in this gentle and deeply insightful book.   *JP Reese*

Glass Animals
by Stephen V. Ramey
ISBN: 978-1-300-66220-4
Originally published January 2013

Ramey takes on the richness of his characters' emotional and physical torment and delivers something morbidly fascinating and keen. A great first collection.   *Kristine Ong Muslim*

Equally irreverent and real, these forty-five flash and micro-sized tales left me feeling as though I'd spent time inside the heads of forty-five different people.

H.G. Estok

Wild: a collection
by Gill Hoffs
ISBN: 978-1-4717-4215-6
Originally published June 2012

Gill Hoffs' writing, fiction and non, swells with the power of life, sometimes life at the expense of other lives, but always animated and alive.   *Ronnie Scott*

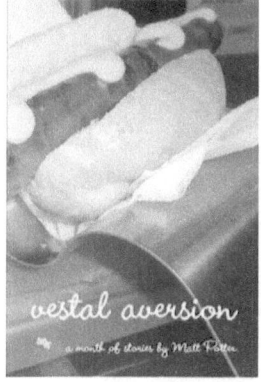

Vestal Aversion
by Matt Potter
ISBN: 978-1-4717-1397-2
Originally published May 2012

His range is wide, exploring topics from extramarital affairs to mean-spirited childhood pranks, and his characters always come through as very human ... entertaining and often thought-provoking.   *Richard Bon*

www.ingramcontent.com/pod-product-compliance
Lightning Source LLC
Chambersburg PA
CBHW031837170626
46807CB00004B/1505